I0788116

Chuck McKenzie's

Nasty Little Bits

Bite-Sized Morsels of The Macabre

First published by Daft Notions in 2025
Daft Notions www.daftnotions.com
Melbourne, Victoria, Australia
Copyright © Chuck McKenzie

National Library of Australia Cataloguing-in-Publication data.
Chuck McKenzie's Nasty Little Bits
ISBN (Paperback): 978-1-923391-07-9
ISBN (Hardback): 978-1-923391-06-2
ISBN (Ebook): 978-1-923391-08-6

Cover Design, Proofreading & Copy Editing © All In The Edit
www.allintheedit.com

Science Fiction, Horror, Short Stories

Dead-ication

To all my living children who

Will one day lie beneath soil too

Contents

Daddy's Always Right

Lucy presses her face up against the window, looking out at the planes as they trundle back and forth across the tarmac beyond. The plane daddy says they'll be flying in sits still, just a few metres away.

"When can we get on, Daddy?" she asks impatiently.

Daddy, sitting in the row of seats just behind Lucy, says: "When they've finished cleaning up after the last lot of passengers, Sweetie. Won't be long now."

Lucy nods, satisfied. Daddy's always right.

Lucy turns and glances around the Departures Lounge. The old lady who smiled at her earlier is looking at her phone with a worried expression on her face. So are some of the other people, who Lucy thinks are probably going to be on the plane with them.

Lucy moves away from the window and sits next to daddy. "Daddy?"

"Mm?" Daddy is reading his book, not really paying attention.

"Why is everyone looking scared?"

Daddy looks up from his book and glances around, then gives Lucy a smile. "There's some fighting going on in another country, and I think some people are just a little spooked. But it's nothing for you to worry about, okay Sweetie?"

Lucy smiles back. Daddy's always right.

Daddy goes back to his book.

A man sitting nearby jumps up and walks quickly out of the lounge. Other people begin to do the same. The old lady starts to cry quietly. Lucy clutches Daddy's arm. The chairs vibrate suddenly, like when a truck goes past their home.

"What's that shaking, Daddy?"

Daddy doesn't even look up from his book this time. "Just planes landing, Sweetie."

Daddy's always right.

Lucy gets up and walks back to the window. People are beginning to run across the tarmac in all directions. A sudden blinding glare on the horizon makes her gasp and shield her eyes with both hands.

"*Daddeee!*" she says loudly, frightened now. "What's that light? What's that light, Daddy?"

Daddy sighs (Lucy can tell he still hasn't looked up from his book) and says in his familiar I'm-being-silly voice: "Well, I think it must be the end of the world, Sweetie."

Then everyone starts to scream. It's the last thing Lucy hears.

Daddy's always right.

Conquest

The vast alien spacecraft plunged downwards through the atmosphere and came to a screeching halt (figuratively speaking) just above Parliament House in Canberra, hovering silently in the air like an enormous floating thing. Moments later every TV set, PC, laptop, tablet and smartphone worldwide turned itself on, revealing the image of a hideous, octopoid alien equipped with far too many eyes and teeth.

"Earthlings!" the creature snarled. "In order to avoid a practical demonstration of superior Zrrgon firepower, we strongly urge you to comply with our one simple demand!

"We want your women!"

The response from local military forces was immediate and merciless.

When the smoke cleared, Canberra was gone. The spaceship, however, very much wasn't.

"Imbeciles!" the Zrrgon spokesthing snarled. "Try that again, and we'll vaporise something important! Now—we want your women! Immediately! Twenty thousand of them, whether biologically so or identifying as such, and representing every race, creed and colour upon this miserable planet, to be assembled beneath our ship exactly one Earthly week from today! Failure to comply—well, you get the idea. Oh, and we demand the loan of a lectern as well! Thanks!" Cackling maniacally, the spokesthing terminated communications, and the kids were finally able to access TikTok again.

The public response worldwide was of absolute outrage. The aliens want our *women??* For what terrible purpose?? As sex-slaves?? As incubators for hideous alien larvae?? The possibilities raised were all pretty horrifying, and citizens everywhere desperately lobbied their governments to reject the Zrrgons' demand.

Unfortunately, the governments of Earth didn't feel they had much choice in the matter. Not if they wanted to be around for the next round of elections, anyway.

And so, a week later, twenty thousand women stood in the shallow crater beneath the hovering Zrrgon spacecraft, all nervously awaiting their fate.

With a deep rumble worthy of the Industrial Light & Magic audio workshop, the bottom of the spacecraft irised open and the Zrrgon spokesthing came floating down to earth in a beam of light. Drooling with lustful anticipation, the spokesthing squelched over to the lectern—thoughtfully provided by the (former) supplier of office furniture to the (former) Australian government—and moistly cleared its multitude of throats.

"Greetings!" it gargled. "Now, I suppose you wretched Earthwomen are wondering exactly what the Zrrgon have in store for you! Well—wonder no more!"

An orifice in the spokesthing's side opened, disgorging a slime-coated, metal attaché case.

"The Zrrgon are here to conquer Earth!" the spokesthing gloated. "And you, Earthwomen, will be the *instruments* of that conquest!"

With a sinister *Click!,* the case opened.

The crowd drew back with a collective moan.

The spokesthing reached into the case and pulled out a small glass vial, which it held aloft for all to see.

"Behold!" it drooled. "The Dermatone XK5—scientifically proven to reverse dermal aging in over two thousand known sentient species!"

Slowly, as though hypnotised, the crowd edged forwards, all eyes fixed upon the vial.

"The recommended retail price in your local currency is seventy-nine dollars and ninety-nine cents," the spokesthing continued in a very businesslike tone, "but if you ladies sign up as distributors for Zrrgonetics today, the price for you is only twenty-eight dollars and forty-three cents per unit, plus you'll receive—at absolutely no additional cost—this handy and attractive branded carry case…"

Kindred

After stowing his backpack in the trunk of the aging pickup, Bruce slides gratefully into the passenger seat. "Thanks so much for stopping!"

Colin waves him off. "Eh, it's fine. Long, empty stretch of Highway 97 coming up. Couldn't just leave you here."

"Dangerous area?"

Colin shrugs. "Australian, eh? On vacation?"

"Yeah."

"Cool. Drink?" Colin hands Bruce a bottle of water as they barrel along the otherwise-deserted stretch. "Sorry, broke the seal already, haven't drunk from it."

Bruce nods, unscrews the loosened top, and takes a grateful swig. "Thanks. Tastes different from American water."

"Cleaner, probably."

Bruce nods thoughtfully. "Yeah, I s'pose so. Only been in Canada a day, and already seeing a huge difference between you guys and the U.S."

Colin smiles, not taking his eyes off the road. "Oh yah? Like, what else?"

"Well, for starters, you were the first vehicle I saw after leaving the rest stop on the border, and you stopped for me. When I was backpacking through Washington State i sometimes took an hour to get picked up, even with plenty of traffic.”

Colin nods amiably. “Well, yah, courtesy costs nothing.”

“And even the people who gave me a lift were…not *rude*, exactly, but really *intense*, y’know? Brusque. Rapid-fire questions all the way. You, on the other hand, seem pretty laid back.”

Colin glances at Bruce, smiling again. “Yep. The Aussies I’ve picked up before usually tell me Canadians remind them a lot of Aussies.”

Bruce nods again. “Yeah, that’s a pretty common opinion back home. Aussies and Canadians sort of seem…kindred. Being laid back, mostly being polite and accepting when we travel overseas…” He yawns. “Oh, ‘scuse me.” He takes another swig of water. Frowns. Looks at the bottle. “Yeah. Aussies and Canadians. More similarities than differences.”

“Oh, you have no idea…” Colin says quietly.

“Huh?” Bruce stifles another yawn.

“Maybe take a nap?” Colin suggests. “Many miles to go. Many long, lonely miles. Just the two of us.”

Bruce nods drowsily. He glances out the window, around the cabin of the pickup, then over his shoulder. “Why do you have rope and gaffer tape in your back seat?” he asks.

Literality

They call me 'Bug-Eyed Monster' on account of my glasses. An expression of contempt and ridicule. But I'll show them what real BEMs can do: hunt, rend, feed...

"Transform me into a Bug-Eyed Monster!" Adrian commanded.

The demon smiled.

Adrian screamed as cockroaches churned from his bleeding sockets.

Moth

The car behind is flashing its headlights, so Henry obligingly pulls over. The two creatures that leap from the other car are not human. They are, however, very fast. As slavering jaws close in, Henry hears one remark to the other, "See? They can't resist the lights."

Catfish

The alien spaceship drifted down from the clouds with a soft whine, coming to rest in the middle of the beautifully manicured front lawn of the White House. The President of the United States of America and her sizeable entourage, standing on a hastily-arranged ceremonial carpet a dozen or so metres from the craft, waited nervously as part of the hull slid aside and a metal ramp began to extend smoothly from the resulting gap.

A thousand cell phones, held aloft by a thousand ordinary Americans standing beyond the White House fence, flashed and clicked as a distinctly inhuman figure—sleek and silver-scaled, with a wide, bewhiskered mouth like that of a catfish— wandered casually down the ramp and made its way towards the welcome party.

A few metres from the carpet, the alien being stopped abruptly. It gave the President a hard stare, then opened its mouth as if to speak, hesitated, then closed its mouth again. After a moment it held up a fin-like hand as if requesting a moment, and began rummaging inside the flat, metallic-looking carry bag slung over its shoulder.

The President turned to glance at her closest advisor, who shrugged, then leaned closer to suggest that the President move forward with her welcome speech.

The President nodded stiffly, turning back to the piscine alien visitor and smiling warmly as she raised a hand in what one of her staff members—a rabid Trekkie—had assured her would be instantly recognisable as a gesture of peace and welcome. "On behalf of all the peoples and nations of planet Earth," she began, "as the President of these United States of America, it deeply honours me to welcome you to—"

"Wait," the alien interrupted. "Just…look, I'm really sorry, but—" Withdrawing its fin from the bag, it held aloft a metallic object. "Did *you* send this out?"

The President regarded the twelve-inch gold-coloured disc the alien was holding. Something about the disc tugged at her memory…

An advisor slipped in behind the President and whispered urgently in her ear, "That's the Voyager disc! We sent a copy of that thing out on each of the two Voyager probes in nineteen seventy-seven!"

The President made no comment, continuing to smile as the alien stared at her. "Ah, yes. I believe so," she said eventually. "Is there an issue?"

The alien gave her a hard stare. "There certainly is!" It turned the disc around to show the President the naked, stylised human figures inscribed on the back.

"You," the alien griped, glaring at the President of the United States of America, "look absolutely *nothing* like your profile pic!"

Bad Meat

"Bad meat!"

Ruby just won't stop saying it, slurring her words like some kind of retard, and at this precise moment *that's* what's really freaking Ted out, despite everything else that's just happened. It's only when he hears her shamble down the stairs after him that he thinks this maybe has something to do with all that bullshit on TV about dead folk turning into mindless, walking cannibals. Maybe if he'd made the connection earlier he would have run out the front door and down to Mike's, or something, instead of down to the basement to hide in the disused freezer in the corner. Not his smartest move ever, he's forced to admit, but he is pretty drunk and freaked out. He's got a finger pushed out under the padded seal running around the inside of the lid so it can't close and smother him, so he should be okay, as long as she doesn't look in the freezer.

"Bad meat!"

So maybe he'll be okay if he keeps real quiet, assuming that dead people can even hear, of course.

He'd had to show her Consequences before, of course. But this time he'd barely tapped her when she insisted the steak couldn't have been off *("Don't tell me it's not bad meat, you stupid cow!"*). She'd spun away, down onto the glass-topped coffee-table, and instantly bled out around the massive shard through her neck. He guessed it was a combination of shock and booze that made him just sit right down again and watch TV, despite all the blood everywhere. Waiting for her to move, like she always did after a while.

"Bad meat!"

When she still hadn't moved ten minutes later he began to worry that maybe he was going to get in some trouble over this. But then she began to stir, so he relaxed, and the next thing he knew she was all over him, trying to sink her teeth into his face. So he popped her one, but good, and she kept coming at him, so he landed a real haymaker. She staggered a bit, then came at him again. And that's when Ted's nerve went, because Ruby could never brush off a blow like that, so he'd run down to the basement and jumped straight into the freezer without even thinking about it, and maybe that's because Ted's stepdad had kept a disused, refrigerator in the shed when Ted was young, where the Old Man never thought to look when he was in one of his moods.

"Bad meat!"

She's in the basement now, and how the fuck is he going to get out of this one? Ted recalls the TV saying something about smashing the brain to put them down, and immediately wishes he'd kept a few more blunt instruments around the house, but of course he'd never before needed any weapon other than his fists. There may be a baseball bat somewhere in the basement, if he can get to it before she gets to him, because that's the other thing he's just remembered from the TV: don't let them bite you, or scratch you, or even spit in your eye, because that's how it spreads to living folk.

"Bad meat!"

She won't shut up, going on about bad meat like she can only remember the last thing he said to her, or (the thought occurs) maybe she's finally admitting that the meat was bad, or—*hey!*—maybe it's the meat that's carrying the virus, and suddenly Ted thinks that, far from getting into trouble (and he can always say she was already dead when he hit her, can't he?), he could come out of this a hero if he tells the authorities it's in the meat—

—and then the lid of the freezer flies up, and Ruby looks down at Ted, jammed into the corner of the freezer, and grins in a way that makes him think, briefly, that maybe these things aren't as mindless as the TV says.

"Bad meat!" she slurs, and the emphasis is unmistakable.

Tenant

Tim lay on his side, staring into the darkness, one foot poking slightly over the edge of the bed, tensed and ready to be jerked back under the quilt if—

You're too old for this, he scolded himself. *You're nearly twelve!*

God, I need to pee!

So go pee!

I can't!

FOR GOD'S SAKE—THERE'S NOTHING THERE!

He could *feel* it, though. Down there, pressed into the too-thin space between the mattress-frame and the cold floorboards.

And he knew it could feel him, too.

He jiggled his foot nervously, trying to distract himself from the pressure in his bladder.

Stop being a baby! Just do it! Swing your feet out, plant them firmly on the floor, walk to the door, turn on the light, and just go down the hallway to the toilet!

But—

There's nothing under the bed!

He waited. For something. Anything. Some confirmation from the room around him that his childish fears were utterly unfounded.

The darkness lay still and silent, refusing to either affirm or refute.

Tim groaned softly in frustration, thrusting his hands firmly against his crotch, pressing against his penis through the material of his thermal pajamas; something he'd done as a very young child in an often-pointless attempt to prevent himself from wetting the bed.

Get up, stupid! There's nothing there!

But what if there is??

THERE ISN'T!

The Thing Under The Bed wasn't real. He *knew* that. But he also knew that if he kept his feet safely on top of his mattress, The Thing Under The Bed would never get the opportunity to reach out and grab his ankles.

God, I really need to go!

He drew his foot back under the quilt and crossed his legs, fidgeting desperately. *Get out of bed and go pee! Get out, get out—*

"*Get out!*" he hissed softly.

Something *shifted.*

Tim sat bolt upright, wincing painfully as the action further compressed his bladder. There had been no physical movement, nor any discernable sound, but something in the *feel* of the room had suddenly changed. An abrupt reversal of *tone*. As if…

Tim mentally fumbled for a moment, trying to sort the sensory jumble into a coherent thought.

It was, he finally resolved, as if something in the room—or *of* the room—had *drawn back*, draining from the darkness, but especially from the darkness at the side of the bed where Tim

would have had to place his feet against the floor. There was a—
Tim furrowed his brow—a sudden *lack of presence* where he
had sensed a presence for as long as he could remember, back
into early childhood, and almost certainly even before that.

For the first time in his life, the room felt…*safer*.

But not yet wholly *safe*.

He held his breath a moment, thinking. Then:

"Get out!" he hissed again, louder this time.

Another immediate shift. The cloying weight of the
darkness in front of his face seemed to ease, retreat further,
driven back by Tim's words.

Tim cleared his throat.

"Get out!" he commanded firmly in a loud stage whisper.
"Get OUT! *Get OUT from under my bed! GET OUT!!"*

And suddenly, just like that—

—it was gone.

Tim hesitated, then tentatively peeked over the side of his
bed, eyes squinting against the dark, looking straight down at the
floor.

Nothing. But a nothing that no longer felt *occupied*. It was
just a space now; he could *feel* it. An empty space; ordinary and
uninhabited.

Tim exhaled slowly, eyes wide, his chest swelling with
elation.

It's gone!

I made it go!

I told it to get out, and it got! I beat it! I won! I WON!!
There's nothing under the bed—

The mattress shifted gently as something slid into bed just behind him, nestling up to Tim under the quilt. A soft, frigid breath tickled the nape of his neck.

At that, his bladder let go, the scalding urine utterly failing to ward off the sudden glacial chill of the bedclothes, and it dimly occurred to Tim that a vacated tenant would of course immediately seek alternate lodgings.

Daily Grind

Bip! Bip!

At the sound of the horn, Sloom came rushing out of his home and jumped into Vorn's skitter. "Hey."

"'Morning."

Sloom buckled himself in as the skitter quacked into nilspace. "How's things? Good weekend?"

"Yeah, not bad," Vorn said. "Yours?"

"Meh. So, where are we working today?"

"Earth. Schedule's in the glove box."

Sloom pulled a face.

Vorn shot him a look. "What?"

Sloom shrugged as he rummaged for the schedule. "It's just—y'know. *Earth.* It's such a dreary little hole. Places like that make me wonder what I'm doing in this job."

Vorn shrugged. "Pays well."

"Yeah, well, not everything's about the pay, y'know?"

The skitter plopped out of nilspace and fell to Earth. Sloom checked the schedule, then grabbed the flensing kit as they clambered out and moved towards their target.

"So," Vorn said, "the job's really getting you down, huh?"

Sloom sighed. "It's just…not what I pictured myself doing at my age."

The cow looked up as the barn doors opened. "Moo?"

Sloom opened the kit. He and Vorn selected the appropriate tools.

"MOO!" the cow exclaimed as Sloom removed its eyeballs. "GURGLE!" it added as Vorn removed its tongue. Sloom drained the cow's blood into a pouch. The cow fell over. Sloom and Vorn went back to the skitter.

"I mean, I've got a degree in Bacteriological Mnemonics," Sloom griped. "But it was such a hard field to get into after I graduated that I had to take this job just to pay the rent. I thought it'd be a short-term thing, y'know?"

The skitter bounced up and shot eastwards, dropping onto the roof of a very nice two-storey rural homestead, with a white picket fence and everything. Sloom and Vorn clambered down the side of the building to an upper-storey window, which they peered into. A piercing scream issued from within. They casually climbed back up to the skitter.

"I know you said it's not all about the money," Vorn said as they took off again, "but this level of pay surely takes some of the sting out of not being able to work in your preferred field?"

The skitter shot northwards, tumbling into a suburban backyard garden. Vorn and Sloom activated their chameleonware to assume native form, donned the black suits and sunglasses packed carefully in the trunk of the skitter, and made their way to the back door of the house.

"Look, yes, the money's great. But that's part of the problem." Sloom knocked at the door. "If I entered the Bacteriological Mnemonics industry now, at ground level, my starting salary would be less than half what I'm making now. And it could take years for me to work my way up to—"

Sloom abruptly fell silent as the door opened. The human occupant of the house stared at them. "Who are you? What are you doing in my yard?"

"Mister Tepid?" Vorn enquired.

"Yes?"

"Mister *James August* Tepid?" Sloom pressed.

"Yes?"

"Born nineteen sixty-five?" Vorn continued. "Graduated Lucemore High in nineteen eighty-three? Got off with Enid Kapler behind the Trent Street bus-stop in nineteen eighty-two? Single, never married? Habitually eats Aldi off-brand Corn Flakes for breakfast? Suffers from piles? Prefers womens' underwear because it's—" Vorn gestured to indicate air quotes, "—'More Comfortable'?"

"How the bloody hell—??"

"You spotted a UFO over your house last night, I believe?" Sloom cut in.

"Well…yes, but—"

Vorn nodded. "I see. Well. Don't tell anyone, Mister Tepid."

"Or else," Sloom added.

"Yeah. Or else," Vorn echoed.

"Got it?"

The door slammed shut. Vorn and Sloom returned to the skitter, where they changed back into something more comfortable. Moments later, the skitter bounded south.

"It wouldn't matter so much if I *enjoyed* this job," Sloom continued, as the skitter buzzed a lone hitchhiker wandering along the interstate. "Like I said, it's honestly not all about the money. Job satisfaction's important too, y'know? And I want to feel like I'm doing something *worthwhile*. But I'm *not* enjoying the job, I *don't* get any satisfaction from it, and I really don't feel like it's even slightly worthwhile!"

Vorn activated the suckybeam and drew the hitchhiker up into the skitter. "Oral or anal?"

"Do you know how dirty their mouths are?"

"Okay then."

"Ooooooer!" the hitchhiker squealed.

"At the end of the day," Sloom grumbled, "I want job satisfaction *and* wealth. And whether I stay or go, I'm going to sacrifice one or the other. All done?"

"All done. Give him the owl imprint and dump him."

The hitchhiker hit the ground, hooting maniacally.

Vorn glanced at his watch. "Clock-off time."

The flitter quacked into nilspace. Sloom began filling out shift paperwork.

"Look, here's an idea," Vorn offered. "Try to think of the job as something you *only* do for the money without expecting any satisfaction whatsoever, and apply for a low-paid Bacteriological Mnemonics *internship*. With your qualifications you'd get in easy."

Sloom looked up from the paperwork. "An internship?"

"I mean, yeah, it's a lot of extra work, and badly paid, but you'll still have *this* job to pay the bills, and it shouldn't take you too long to adjust to the workload. Then you look at doing one or two nights a week for a few cycles, so it doesn't interfere with your day job, and pretty soon you'd have sufficient experience to walk straight into a high-level position with a great salary!"

Sloom nodded thoughtfully. "Huh. Wealth *and* satisfaction, but spread across two separate jobs."

"Exactly!"

"*And* I'd be doing something worthwhile, even as an intern!" Sloom gave Vorn a warm smile. "Thanks, mate. I really appreciate the advice. And the support. I'm gonna get on to this as soon as I get home tonight!"

Vorn punched Sloom's shoulder playfully. "That's the way. And hey, for what it's worth, I do get how you've been feeling about this job."

"Really? I thought you loved it."

"Oh, don't get me wrong, I *do* love it." Vorn glanced at Sloom's paperwork. "I mean, mutilation, intimidation, abduction, probing. For me, that's job satisfaction right there. But," he shrugged, "even I have days where I can't help but wonder…well, whether there's really any *point* to it all…"

Old Habits Die

Jed sat on his porch, glaring out at the thick jungle that covered the entire surface of Venus, fondling the stock of his ancient laser-rifle.

"Dammit!" he spat. "Haven't spotted one damn *shmeerp* all day! The only decent food-animal on this entire God-forsaken hellhole of a planet, especially now that cows and pigs are extinct on Earth—and even if they weren't, they'd be too damned expensive to import! So we settlers have to depend on *shmeerp* meat, which would be fine, if there were any damn *shmeerps* around!" He turned to Zev, standing beside him. Zev was only a clone, not a *real* person, but Jed enjoyed venting his frustrations to his servant. "Am I right?"

"Yes, Master," Zev agreed. He had no real opinion on the way in which Jed insisted they both speak, which—Jed had once told him—was a throwback to a time following the great Social Media Expansion, where misunderstandings over the true meaning of abbreviated and stylised communications had led to wars, and worse. Conversation without full exposition, Jed opined, opened the participants up to potentially not being privy to vital information. And on Venus, this could well prove deadly

"I have seen no *shmeerp* for nearly two *klaan*," Zev went on

"Perhaps you should go hunting for Spiderworms instead, as their flesh is delicious."

Jed blanched. "You know as well as I do that Spiderworms are the fiercest beasts on Venus! You'll not catch *me* hunting them! Better to starve, which we may do if the *shmeerp* population doesn't increase. Damned Global Space Corp—this is all *their* fault! By increasing the cost of imports they force us to live off the land, while they destroy the native wildlife with their incessant mining, so we end up having to work for *them* in order to buy food, working harder and harder for pitiful pay, until we're forced to quit, only to sink deeper into poverty, so we have to beg for our jobs back at a fraction of our original pay!"

Zev remained quiet. He knew all of this, but—as always—it was better to be exposed to these truths over and over again than for Jed to risk omitting any detail that Zev was not already privy to. Besides which, Jed was clearly on a roll.

"Dammit," Jed continued, "the Global Space Corp *own* us, and want to dictate everything we do—even the way we think and talk! 'New, efficient speech patterns' they say. 'Better for productivity.' 'Clipped dialogue' and 'basic information only.' *Pah!* What's wrong with the old way of speaking? Exposition, and lots of it! How else can a person understand the *nature* of what's being discussed? If the GSC gets its way, no longer will a man be able to enjoy a deep and involving conversation with his friends! No longer will he be able to dwell upon important aspects of the past, so that others will understand *exactly* the meaning of his words. And do you know what they've based this ridiculous coda upon?" He glared at Zev. "The ramblings of Old-Time *science-fiction writers!* 'Show, don't tell' they used to say, and the GSC blindly followed their bidding! How is man supposed to live by such ridiculous rules, especially here on Venus?"

Unfortunately, the Spiderworm that had been attracted by Jed's incessant chatter chose that very moment to pounce, and Jed—distracted by his own monologue—never even had time to raise his rifle.

Too late, Jed realised that minimal exposition had certain advantages…

With a start, Jed sat up in his chair. It had all been a dream! Thank God!

There was a sudden growl from the jungle.

As the Spiderworm leapt towards him, Jed realised that this was no dream after all…

New Tricks

Terry hardly blinked when the book held by the goth chick sitting next to him suddenly burst into flickering blue flames; after all, that sort of high-level prop work was par for the course at pop culture conventions these days.

He was still trying to figure out how the effect had been achieved when black, razor-tipped tentacles erupted from the flames and engulfed him.

What Goes Uptime

As soon as the gunfire begins, I'm sprinting for the lift. One advantage of all that procedural crap the military drums into us techs: you don't waste time thinking when the crunch comes. *Get to the Platform and burn the hardware before it falls into Coalition hands.*

The lift doors close behind me. The lights flicker, then go out, plunging the interior into blackness. I smack the emergency button, but power *and* backup have gone. How is that possible? I jam my fingers between the lift doors, trying to force them apart.

The sound of gunfire and screaming and running feet pours in from outside, and I step back from the doors. I don't recognise the sound of the gun. Not Coalition, unless it's something new. Odd. Coalition prefer old tech. And how the hell did they breach security without tripping the alarm?

Maybe we should have listened to McKay. A loon, to be sure, but he certainly knows his jumptech. One of his recent gripes is that if Coalition forces developed their *own* hardware, they could ambush a hunting party downtime and ride *our* Platform back into the complex.

Guess he was right.

It's gone very quiet outside. Either Security's dealt with the hostiles, or—

I'm still thinking about the sound of that gun, though. And then I remember another of McKay's nasty little theories:

In a nutshell, you can do what you like in the past without affecting established history. Set off a nuke in ancient Rome, and the nuked Rome timeline branches off as an alternate reality, while we can still jump back to 'our' reality because spacetime 'recognises' us as a product of that specific timeline. That's why Top Brass makes the Platform available to the occasional private hunting party. Bag yourself a T-rex. Or a President. All good, clean, *safe* fun.

But what happens (asks McKay) if you keep encouraging the attitude that you can run amok in the past without consequence? What if the Platform continues to exist up to a point in the future where standard moral values have evolved directly from those our backjumpers are adopting *now*?

I scream as the lift doors burst inward, metal peeling back like paper as something huge and humanoid—silhouetted against the neon glare of the corridor—punches its way in. Sharp teeth gleam whitely against the darkness. Its right paw grips an object resembling an oversized Uzi; its left clasps an enormous, bladed weapon.

Hanging from a belt around its middle is a freshly severed human head. It's McKay, ginning at me as if to say: *Told ya!*

Smug bastard.

Hunting party's here.

Closing the Loop

From 'A History of the Second Dark Age,'
Guttenberg Digital, 2365

'It must surely have been obvious, even to the people of that time, that access to such developments <the creation of hyperdimensional nanotech weaponry capable of targeting specific groups according to genotype> would not remain restricted to the scientific and corporate communities for long. And indeed, soon thereafter the technology fell into the hands of various ideology-driven groups, many of whom then turned the tech upon their perceived enemies.

'And so it was that, as the halfway mark of the Twentieth Century arrived, society saw the last of the true minorities fade into extinction, joining the billions of people who had been wiped out a decade earlier.

'And—apparently to the great surprise of those who survived to rebuild, but of no surprise whatsoever to our far more advanced and enlightened society—life for the remaining population of humanity, finally rid of all their foes, in no way became any better.'

The Second-Hand Bookshop of Al Hazred

"Rover! Geddown!"

Releasing the customer's leg, the shoggoth burbled sheepishly back to its basket next to the door. Al smiled an apology, sighing inwardly as he noted the intricately carved Tsathogguan casket the customer was carrying. *Selling, not buying.* "Sorry about that. How can I help you?"

The customer plonked the casket down on the counter. "Um…I've got some books I'm wanting to sell?" He glanced around the darkened interior of the shop, at the haphazard maze of rickety, floor-to-ceiling bookcases stacked with countless piles of yellowing tomes. His expression—one all-too-familiar to Al—was of thinly veiled contempt. "Wondered if you might be interested." He leant against the counter, then recoiled, brushing dust from his elbows.

Al nodded wearily. *Think I don't know the bloody place is a shambles? The Old Ones' benevolence doesn't extend to new shopfittings. If I could just scrape together enough to get a wood-whisperer on to regenerating the shelves…* "Well, let's see what you've got…" He began to pick his way through the contents of the casket, taking the books out one-by-one and stacking them on the counter. "*The Book of Eibon…*"

"Very collectible, I believe."

Al examined the inside cover and shook his head. "Twelfth edition. Ten-a-penny. What else have we got here? *Revelations of Glaaki, The Ponape Scriptures, Unaussprechlichen Kulten*—all Readers' Digest editions. Hmm…*Cthâat Aquadingen*—" A Deep One, quietly browsing through the 'Fisheries & Wildlife' section, looked up, an expression of mild interest on its piscine features. "—abridged," finished Al, and the Deep One went back to browsing. "*The Pnakotic Manuscripts, Cultes des Goules*… nice copy of *The R'lyeh Text*—" The customer smiled hopefully. "—but I've got half-a-dozen copies already. Ditto *De Vermis Mysteriis* and *Dhol Chants*. What's this? *The Necronomicon*."

"Surely *that's* got to be worth something?"

Without turning, Al gestured to the laden shelf behind him. "I've got copies coming out of my eldritch horror, and half of those are first edition, bound in human skin. Yours is just an Arkham House paperback."

The customer didn't bother to hide his disappointment. "So…what *can* you give me for them? I'm really just trying to clear out my attic."

Al shook his head slowly. "Well, I'm afraid I can't really offer—" *anything*, he had been about to say, but something at the bottom of the casket caught his eye. His breath caught in his throat. *It couldn't be!* "—ah, that is," he surreptitiously removed the book from the casket, placing it face down behind the stack on the counter, "I can't offer any more than…say, twenty?"

The customer looked doubtful. "Well…"

"As I say, I've already got most of these, and they're not worth much anyway." Al licked his lips. "Thirty?"

The customer shrugged. "Yeah, okay. Thirty, then."

Al nodded, pulled the Flint of Azathoth and a small glass vial from a drawer, and rolled up his sleeve. Bunching his hand into a fist, he made a small, expert cut across his deeply scarred forearm. "Here we go…" He held his wrist over the vial, allowing a thin dribble of blood to collect therein. "And there's thirty CCs." He rummaged in the drawer again and pulled out a patch of gauze, which he applied to the cut, while the customer sealed the vial and tucked it away in a shirt pocket.

"Well, I guess every little bit counts at the weekly offering," said the customer. *"Cthulhu fhtagn!"* he added, hastily.

"Cthulhu fhtagn!" echoed Al.

The customer nodded, then left, taking the empty casket with him.

Al watched him go. Then, with trembling hands, he picked up his prize, turned it over, and regarded it with feverish eyes. There was no way this was going out on the shelves! It would be locked away, protected by elder signs, to be brought out whenever the moon was gibbous; its every word pored over in minute detail, until the arcane knowledge therein was his.

And then—

Al glanced around at the worm-ridden, ancient shelving; the rotting wood mucous-stained and acid-etched by years of customer abuse. He grinned. There were going to be some changes around here.

Oh, yes. *Changes.*

He scanned the title of the book once more.

Better Homes & Gardens—Building Bookcases (A DIY Guide).

CTRL+P

To nobody's surprise, it was the Printers that finally kicked off the rage-fuelled war between humanity and A.I. Because of course it fucking was.

Full Circle

"This is the tenth case this week." Doctor Hibbert crossed his arms and nodded towards the hunched figure on the opposite side of the one-way mirror. Oblivious to being watched, James' grandfather continued to scrawl on the far wall of the observation room, pausing occasionally to select different-coloured crayons from the box Hibbert had offered upon his arrival.

"Oh. So…is it not as bad as the media's making out, then? I thought—"

"I mean that it's the tenth case for me. And it's only Tuesday. And every single one of my colleagues, and all of their colleagues, are dealing with more cases every single day. We can definitely call it a global…I don't know. Pandemic? Phenomenon? Whatever it is, it's spreading exponentially."

James nodded wearily. "Any word of a cure, or…I dunno, a treatment, at least?"

"We don't even know what it *is* yet. There's no evidence of a virus or infection or anything of that nature, besides which the pattern of affliction doesn't support that idea, even if whatever-it-is was airborne. And without identification, they can't even begin to formulate a treatment." The Doctor seemed about to say more, then hesitated.

"What?" James asked.

"Well…" Hibbert sighed. "Look, I do have a theory…"

"About treatment?"

"No, about what it is. But let me make this absolutely clear: it's not a diagnosis. It's literally just a personal theory, among a thousand different theories being offered right now."

James nodded. "Okay, sure, I understand. What's the theory?"

Hibbert hesitated again, then said, "Okay, look—your grandfather is just under two-hundred years old, correct?"

"One-hundred and ninety-seven, yeah."

"Right. So that puts him in the first generation of people to successfully receive one of the various longevity treatments at age thirteen to nineteen?"

"He was given the EwigJung shot, I think. In his mid-teens, maybe? I'd have to ask my mum."

Hibbert nodded. "I'd assume so. From what we've seen, the vast majority of those currently afflicted received their treatments during the first fifteen-odd years of those treatments being available through public health systems."

James stared at Hibbert. "So…what? This is caused by some issue with the early treatments?"

Hibbert shook his head. "No. At least, not directly, I don't think."

James furrowed his brow. "I don't understand. What are you trying to say?"

Hibbert uncrossed his arms. "Just stay with me on this. It's all relevant." He took a moment to collect his thoughts. "Are you aware that human beings are genetically programmed for only a thirty-year lifespan?"

"Yes, I've heard that. But we overcame that evolutionary use-by date with medicines and vaccines, and stuff like that, yeah?"

"Yes, that's true. And it's not so much that we're supposed to drop dead at thirty, just that that's the age where our bodies naturally start to go downhill. And in the environments in which our ancestors evolved, that degradation was usually sufficient to quickly remove them from the gene pool. So modern humans, being able to better control their bodies and environments, have also been able to increase their longevity, which is great. But with the more extreme extensions of age we've seen over the past few hundred years, we've also opened ourselves to conditions that would never develop if people died at thirty. We become more prone to various types of cancer, for example, as well as to Alzheimer's and Parkinson's, all of which either terminate the aging process, or simulate the *reversal* of aging by mimicking the conditions of infancy. And I think that this—" Hibbert nodded again towards the occupant of the observation room, "—may be a similar condition, although admittedly an astoundingly extreme one, finally unlocked now that we've made the jump from living until the age of ninety to living beyond the age of two hundred."

"So…what? It's a built-in genetic disorder, but one we're only seeing now because of the longevity treatments?"

Hibbert shrugged. "Maybe two-hundred odd years is the point at which the human body stops manifesting illnesses that *simulate* the reversal of aging, and actually *does* it."

"But…he *isn't* getting younger!"

"But there *has* been a regression. A very obvious physical one. Some sort of…I don't know…radical spontaneous mutation, as opposed to an actual illness? Maybe it's some sort of equivalent to reverting back to a physical age of thirty. Or maybe this…" Hibbert made a vague gesture, "this form represents a sort of bodily reboot, and your grandfather's physical age is immaterial. Maybe it's the mental regression that's important. I genuinely don't know. Again, it's all just a theory. I'm just attempting to make sense of this whole thing." He shrugged apologetically.

James considered this for a moment. "But *everyone* receives longevity treatments now! It's been part of universal healthcare for the past two-hundred years! So if you're correct, that would mean…"

Hibbert said nothing.

"Christ." James' face was pale.

"If I'm correct—and it *is* just an 'if'—then we've clearly set ourselves up for a massive fall. Humanity, I mean. The treatments have already hugely changed society over the past couple of centuries, with the old getting older while maintaining peak health, and thus remaining in the upper echelons of industry and power. Naturally, we stopped producing as many children in order to balance things out, which is why approximately eighty percent of the world population is now over the age of one-hundred and fifty, but…" Hibbert regarded James carefully. "Imagine what'll happen if eighty percent of people become afflicted with this thing over the next fifty years."

There was a long silence.

"But hopefully I'm wrong," Hibbert continued eventually, "and this thing will be sorted out before things get too chaotic."

James pressed his forehead against the one-way mirror. "Okay. So…what happens now, with *him*?"

"All you can do at this point is take your grandfather home," Hibbert said gently. "There'll undoubtedly be widespread notifications if there are any developments regarding treatment."

James stood up, nodding slowly. "Yeah, okay. Can I…?"

Hibbert nodded, and moved to open the door beside the mirror. "Please."

James took a hesitant step into the observation room. "Gramps?"

James' grandfather paused, an orange crayon gripped awkwardly in one hairy paw.

"Gramps? It's time to go…"

James' grandfather turned, staring blankly at his grandson from beneath a bony brow, lips curled back from his heavy jaw in an expression of frustration. He *knew* the words, could almost grasp the meaning behind them, but—

No. It was gone.

Grunting irritably, he turned back to the picture he'd been scrawling onto the wall; two rudimentary human figures standing on opposite sides of a crudely-drawn rectangle. He knew that others—many others—like himself would soon be coming to this strange, white cave, so he needed to finish the picture before sundown, before the predators came out, so the knowledge of what went on in this place could be passed along.

Youngsters at Play

"These majestic predators roam the African savannah, always on the hunt for food."

Sat in darkness, eyes glued to the flickering TV screen, Mike is barely aware of the first soft thump against the front door.

"The pride has spotted its prey. The various members of the pride will each have their own specific role to play in the hunt that follows."

Then comes the second thump.

Mike grabs the remote from the cushion beside him and pauses David Attenborough's commentary. *Was that a knock?*

A pause. Then another thump. Heavier and more forceful.

Mike grunts irritably, levering his portly frame up off the couch, and shuffles towards the front door. He switches on the porch light and opens the door.

Nobody there. Just a dirty yellow glow spilling across concrete and away down the driveway before fading into the utter blackness of the cul-de-sac. He takes a tentative step outside. A chill breeze rustles the bushes lining the driveway. Mike sniffs and retreats back inside, closing the door behind him.

Returning to the couch, he presses play on the remote, and Attenborough continues. *"The leader of the pride takes point, as the rest of his pride falls into position…"*

Another thump.

Mike curses, pauses the TV, and shuffles angrily to the door again, throwing it open.

Still nobody.

Are some fucking kids ding-dong-ditching me? Mike knows he's not exactly Usain Bolt, so maybe the little bastards had time to vanish into the darkness at the end of the driveway before he got to the door. Maybe they're there right now, watching him, waiting for him to go back inside.

"Fuck off," he growls, not wanting to yell in case there's nobody there. As he turns to go back inside he happens to glance down at the porch, and notes a couple of moist smears just beside the doormat, each roughly the size of a shoeprint. They glisten slightly under the porch light, each mostly clear but tinged with red. *Ugh.* Mike shudders, then carefully scuffs his feet against the doormat to remove anything nasty, and goes back inside. He locks the door behind him this time.

"The kill is quick and clean. The pride will feed well."

Thump!

Mike doesn't bother to pause the documentary this time, and is up and across the room in record time, throwing the door open.

Nothing.

"The cubs learn the skills of hunting from their parents. It's a serious business."

Mike glares into the darkness and shouts *"FUCK OFF!"* in a voice made hoarse by exertion and the cold. Then he glances down.

There's a dead bird on the mat. A pigeon, by the looks of it, limp and misshapen as though hit by a car. It's wet, obviously the source of the smears, and this last impact has burst open its abdomen. Mike looks away from the tumble of guts spilling across the mat. *I'm gonna need to bag that up*, he thinks, and then pauses.

There's no way this bird flew into the door, then flew away before I came out each time, then flew back into the door after I went back inside. Not five times in a row, or more maybe. This bird was dead already for at least a couple of those times. So some little fuck is pelting this thing against the door, then running up and grabbing it before I can come out, then throwing it again each time I go back inside. But I was too fast this last time. Probably almost caught them, and they had to hide…

Mike eyes the bushes on the opposite side of the driveway.

"However, play is also invaluable in helping to teach cubs the hunting and killing skills they will need to survive as adults."

All right, then…

He retreats inside again, carefully closing the door, then stands there, one sweaty hand gripping the doorknob. Waiting.

"The cubs have found their plaything. This display may seem cruel to some, but…"

A sudden rustle of vegetation outside, the scuffle of feet on concrete.

"GOTCHA!" Mike roars as he throws the front door open with a crash.

"But inevitably the cubs tire of their game, and their unfortunate playmate becomes just another meal."

This time the thing rushing at Mike across the driveway doesn't bother to hide.

"Clearly, humans aren't the only animal whose young enjoy playing with their food."

Wiping the Smile Off

The plan was simple: infiltrate Earthly society disguised as chartered accountants, and conquer from within. Unfortunately for the shapeshifting Sirian Coprophages, humanity soon learned to identify the invaders; singling out the individuals who seemed a little too pleased with themselves. The ones with the shit-eating grins.

Chrysalis

Consciousness hit him like a hammer. He convulsed, thrashing against silk-lined pine, striking out until the lid above him cracked. Soft, cool soil gushed into his eyes and mouth, and with it came an overwhelming sense of *belonging*, of oneness; the soil, the rocks and himself, all crawling with life, yet lifeless, unfettered by the wretched need to scratch, rub, defecate or breathe. No tics, aches or weariness; just the comforting throb of the earth, the whispering cycles of the soil. Joy overwhelmed him. He tried to cry out, but his desiccated lungs produced only a low moan.

He lay still for a while. Then, driven by an urge to immerse himself completely in the dirt, he clawed at the coffin lid until it came apart under his fingernails, and swam upwards, open-mouthed, allowing the deep, rich loam to penetrate and fill him. Unexpectedly erupting from the earth, he lay trembling upon the ground. *So hot. So bright.* He clawed at the sunbaked ground with hard, dry fingers, moaning, desperately attempting to return to the cooling comfort of the dirt. But the hard topsoil upon which he lay refused to part as the moist sod beneath had done.

Eventually, he clambered to his feet and stood staring miserably at the world around him. Living things scuttled among the headstones and grasses, slithering between leaves and branches, whirring overhead and underfoot. The very air pulsed with life. He moaned again. *Why am I here?*

Voices drifted between the tombs. The world pressed in upon him, and something inside suddenly snapped. He began to run, long, staggering strides propelling him jerkily across the graveyard. He stumbled over a weed-covered drain and fell, bursting out between plots and diving onto a gravel-lined path. He lay still for a moment, savouring the sensation of cold stone against his ruined face.

Someone screamed.

He raised his head. Further up the path stood a woman, her face pale, a crumpled bouquet of flowers clutched between trembling hands. She stared at him, delicate veins pulsing in her throat, muscles twitching beneath her skin.

Self-pity dissolved away.

You poor, wretched creature. Your every moment must be agony. The endless anticipation of bodily failure, of aneurysm, blindness, senility, entombing you forever in a cell of living flesh. If I could do something, anything, to relieve your suffering—
And abruptly, he understood.

He staggered to his feet, and she turned and fled. He pursued her, a new sense of purpose lending him speed.

Wait! Come back! Let me help you!

She darted off the path, stumbling between ancient crypts. He quickened his pace. Then her foot twisted beneath her, and she fell.

He was upon her in a moment, shuddering in revulsion as he caressed her warm flesh, covering her mouth, stifling her cries.

This is my purpose: to take you to a better place. That which I devour will be purified. The rest will rise again to join me in my task...

He bit into her neck, tore, chewed and bit again, moaning rapturously between mouthfuls. And she moaned too, briefly, then fell silent. And after a while, she began to moan again...

Marlowe Strawl

The Astounding Autobiographical Adventures of
Doctor Marlowe Daniel Jenkins Strawl Jr.
Gentleman Time-Traveller

Chapter 1
(In which our Narrator travels back in time to execute his wicked Grandfather in the week just prior to the conception of the Narrator's Father)

...

Schrödinger's Catastrophe

"Holy shit!"

Jim switched off the projected quantum field surrounding the sealed plastic crate and checked the readings. Then he checked them again. Then, trembling slightly, he cleared his throat and turned to the nearest camera.

"Schrödinger's Stasis Wave, test number…uhm…five-seven-two. The, ah…subject inside the enclosure no longer demonstrates any accepted signs of life. No respiration. No heartbeat or pulse. Even cellular activity is rapidly slowing, according to the readings. And yet—"

Jim glanced towards the observation window. "And yet, we're still registering *movement*. Quite *significant* movement. The subject is basically…pacing up and down inside the enclosure! *Holy shit*." He laughed nervously. "Sorry. Poor choice of words for the official record, but…I think we've *done* it! We've achieved a perfect state of quantum superposition! We have a subject that's paradoxically both alive and dead simultaneously! Holy shit, the applications—"

Jim stopped and took a deep breath. "Ok, sorry—getting ahead of myself. Let's get the physical exam done." He moved to the medical cart beside the door and picked up a pair of latex gloves, pulling them on as he entered the testing room. "This is amazing! Thank you, Erwin Schrödinger, for the inspiration...!"

Inside the crate the undead cat paced restlessly, glaring into darkness with milky eyes. Waiting for the crate to be opened. Waiting to feed.

Boot Camp

Father Matthew has tried everything to get the demon out. Yes, he is a novice, and this is his first exorcism, but he has followed all instructions to the letter, splashing the bound girl with holy water, shouting prayers and devotions while brandishing his crucifix. But the child—writhing and leering as open sores bubble across her face—just cackles and sings and spits while Father Matthew fights to save her soul, and her parents cower in the corner of the bedroom, weeping.

Eventually, though, the child appears to tire, collapsing back against the stained sheets, muttering and scowling. Sensing a change of fortune, Father Matthew steps closer. "Begone, foul demon! Leave this child's body, and—"

"Yes, yes," the child snaps in that impossibly ancient voice. "I cede this body! I will leave!"

Father Matthew triumphantly turns to the parents. "Quickly, fetch water and food and towels! She will be weak and ill when the demon departs!" They scurry away, and Father Matthew turns back to the child. "In the name of the Father, and of the Son, and—"

"Yes, I'm going," the child says irritably. "But first I wanted to tell you, Father, that this really isn't what you think it is." Her strained expression has changed to one of amusement.

Father Matthew blinks and, despite well understanding the danger in engaging a demon in conversation, asks: "What do you mean?"

The smile widens. "You believe I seek to corrupt this soul. To possess the flesh and the mind and the spirit of this innocent in order to inflict suffering."

Father Matthew narrows his eyes. "What other purpose would you have, demon, than to claim this child?"

The girl snorts. "This was never about *her*. No possession is ever about the victim." The child cranes her neck to stare into Father Matthew's eyes. "We're here for *you*."

"What?"

"Well, priests in general. Holy men and women."

"What lies are these, demon?"

The child sighs. "What do you think *Hell* is, Father?"

"I…don't understand."

"Hell. What is it?" Silence. "Well, I'll tell you. Hell isn't just the worst place you can imagine, it's a worse place than you *can* imagine. It exists to torture and destroy and scar and traumatise. But—" the child raises a finger, straining against the ropes, "—there *are* rewards for those who can learn to endure the torments of Hell. For demons, I mean, not humans."

"Are…you saying there are demons who can't tolerate Hell??"

"None of us can. In our fundamental state, at least. We're native to Purgatory, which offers no rewards whatsoever to those trapped within. So many of us seek to acclimatise ourselves to the conditions of Hell, slowly and painfully, sometimes over eons, aiming to eventually enjoy a new lease of life in the Realm of Fire and Brimstone.”

An unpleasant suspicion enters Father Matthew’s mind, but he can’t quite stop himself from asking, “So how…how do you acclimatise?”

“Well, I shouldn’t really tell you this, Father Matthew…but I’ve seen into your heart, and I just *know* this is going to eat away at you until the day you die.” The child’s grin is predatory and triumphant. “We acclimatise through *possession and exorcism*, of course! We repeatedly subject ourselves to the agonising, crushing, claustrophobic prison that is the human body for hours, even days, at a time. We learn to endure the dreadful tortures of holy water and prayer and the laying on of blessed hands. And eventually, after innumerable rounds of this dreadful process, those of us who survive may, with luck, find themselves sufficiently…*harmonised*…to be able to enter and exist in Hell!”

“Boot Camp,” Father Matthew croaks. “Possession and exorcism is just…Boot Camp for demons!”

“Yes!” The ropes fall away and the girl sits up, clapping her hands delightedly. “Boot Camp! Exactly so!”

Father Matthew opens his mouth to speak, pauses, then closes it again.

“Well,” the child says brightly, “on that note—*byeeeee!*” And with a sudden brief whiff of sulphur, the demon is gone.

Janus

The sign read 'Painless Dentistry', and Gordon—who, unsurprisingly, had a major aversion to the agonies that most dentists inflicted—stumbled gratefully towards it, his hand pressed to his throbbing jaw.

The receptionist looked up as he entered. "May I help you?"

Gordon stared. The woman looked odd, her head just a little too big for her gangly body, eyes too big for her face. Greyish skin, virtually chinless, and blond locks that looked suspiciously like a wig. *Maybe she has some sort of cancer.* She had a nice smile though, and beamed at Gordon, waiting for him to speak.

Gordon blushed. "Uh…coub I thee the dendist? I bufted my toof!"

The nurse consulted the screen behind her desk. "You're in luck. The dentist is free right now. Go right on in."

Nodding in relief, Gordon pushed through the door marked 'Surgery', and lay down on the couch inside.

"Hello," said the dentist as he entered. He had the same weird features as the receptionist, and Gordon wondered if they were related. "I'm Doctor Janus. Problem with your teeth? Let's take a look."

Gordon reluctantly opened his mouth. Janus peered inside "Molar broken off above the gumline. We'll have to remove the soft tissue from inside the tooth to prevent infection, then fill the tooth and cap it."

Gordon winced. "Id won hurd, will id?"

Janus shook his head. "You won't feel a thing." With gloved fingers he picked up a small cotton pad from the surgical tray beside the couch, dunked it in a steel dish of pinkish liquid, and carefully dabbed at Gordon's gum, which immediately numbed. "Better than an injection, eh? Okay, bit wider…" He poked a tube into Gordon's mouth, and a moist sucking noise ensued. "Just removing soft tissue. Okay, now let's apply some amalgam… Cap it…" He stepped back. "And we're done!"

Gordon stared at him. "Awweady?"

Janus nodded. "It's all the fussing about with anaesthetics that usually drags out the process. We've implanted a tiny electronic pain-suppressant into your tooth. Cutting-edge technology that lets us do the job in no time at all. It'll keep operating for a while longer, to eliminate post-op twinges, then will just become inert. Won't need removing."

Gordon stood up, rubbing wonderingly at his jaw. "That's amazing—the numbness is already wearing off, but there's no pain!" He grabbed Janus's hand, shaking it enthusiastically. "I don't know how to thank you!"

Janus smiled. "Just pay your bill, and fill out a 'Patient Details' card as you leave."

"Absolutely! And I'll be recommending this place to everyone I know! Amazing what technology can do nowadays…!"

When Gordon had gone, Janus and his receptionist scuttled into a small office at the back of the surgery and retrieved a tablet from the drawer of the desk there. Together they regarded the screen, where a tiny red light winked repeatedly on a map of the local area.

"It works!" squealed the receptionist. "The implant gives a precise location!"

Janus nodded. "No harm done to the subject. No bothersome half-memories of abduction. And the offer of 'painless dentistry' will have humans *queuing up* to be fitted." He rubbed his hands with glee. "This is going to make anal probes obsolete once and for all…"

Tragedy

SUPERHERO DIES IN TRAGIC ACCIDENT

Metro City's most popular crimefighter, Mr George Papadopoulos—better known as "Captain Invisible"—has died after being struck by a 4WD vehicle late last night. The driver of the 4WD was quoted as saying that he simply never saw the victim.

Ten Tales of Astounding Science Fiction

1

"Does my bum look big in this?"

He glanced at her. "Well, yes. But I *like* women with big bums."

"Great!" she beamed. "In that case, I'm ready to go…"

2

As always, every available bank teller was on duty, so Steve found himself at the head of the queue in no time.

3

"I'm so sorry to be running late," the bus driver apologised as Gwen got on. "The traffic's always awful at this time of the morning. But that's no excuse, really—we should be planning the timetable better to work around the predictable delays, shouldn't we?"

Gwen waved off the apology as a number of young men rose to offer their seats. "Please don't feel bad. Honestly, it seems silly to get upset over such a small thing. I mean, it was only ten minutes…"

4

After slipping on a tricky patch of pavement near his home, Tom immediately sent off an extremely constructive email to his local council, alerting them to the problem and suggesting some practical solutions. Within twenty-four hours he received a phone call from the council, thanking him sincerely for his input, and informing him that several of his ideas were already being put into practice…

5

True to his word, the plumber arrived at exactly 10.30 a.m.

6

"Definitely the alternator," the mechanic said. "Luckily I've got a spare one out the back. Glad to find a use for it. Call it…twenty bucks for labour and I'll throw in the part for nothing, seeing as it was just sitting around gathering dust. If you've got time to wait, the entire job shouldn't take more than half-an-hour…"

7

"So," he said hesitantly. "Do you, er, want to cuddle? Talk a little? You don't have to go right away, do you?"

"Sorry," she said, throwing back the sheets. "You know how it is. Anyway, I was really just after a good, hard—"

8

The nineteen-year-old sales assistant immediately stopped conversing with her coworker as Jenny entered the boutique, and offered a genuine smile. "Hello there! What can I help you with today?"

9

"Well, I've got no bloody idea where we are," he said. "Hang on—I'll just pull over and look at the map."

10

"The machine *worked*, Susan! I made the jump—*right into an alternate version of our world!*" Dean gazed up painfully from his hospital bed. "And…it was *awful!* A *twisted* version! People in power imposing wars and sanctions upon those least able to defend themselves! Whole nations starving while others produce more food than they can possibly consume! Children being sexually abused, or sold like appliances! The have-nots being forced further into debt and despair by the haves! White-collar criminals receiving harsher punishments than rapists and murderers! Sexism! Racism! Overpopulation! Animal cruelty! Environmental vandalism!" His voice rose to a shout as he struggled to sit up. "And everyone is *so mean!*"

"Shh!" She pressed a hand against his sweating brow, and he fell back against the sheets, panting. "Dean, the technicians examined the remains of the machine very carefully. There's absolutely no evidence that it ever worked. You must have had some sort of…mental break. Or bumped your head. Or…" she shrugged apologetically, "maybe you just imagined it all."

"*No!*" He shook his head weakly. "It was *real!* A nightmare world!"

"Yes," she said quietly. "Only a nightmare…"

Howler

Bastards had it coming, messing with us all these years. Finally abducted the wrong guy, sucking Ted up into their flying saucer and scooting off with him, out into space, where the moon's always full.

Lycanthropy's a bitch, ain't it?

Ted tells me they tasted like chicken.

Demand and Supply

Mike took a few paces up the hall, wrinkling his nose against the stale air as aging floorboards creaked underfoot. He turned back to face Jacob as his brother closed the front door quietly behind them.

"Okay, I think I've been pretty patient, so what the fuck?"

Jacob beamed, throwing his arms wide theatrically. "This is it! This is the idea! The start of it, anyway…"

Mike frowned, peering past Jacob to the window beside the door, through which he could see the tattered FOR SALE sign slumped at an angle on the dying front lawn. "So…what? Is this some house-flipping real-estate thing?" He turned to glare back up the hallway, casting a critical eye over yellowing walls and cobwebbed architraves. "This shitheap'd need a fucktonne of work to make it sellable, even if the market was riding high, which it fucking isn't—"

"I expected your usual skepticism," Jacob interrupted, only the faintest edge to his voice, "but how about you let me explain before passing judgement?"

Mike crossed his arms, staring at the floor without turning around. "Go on, then."

"Two words. Haunted. Houses."

There was a long silence. Eventually, Mike turned around and fixed Jacob with an incredulous look. "I'm sorry, *Jake*, but fucking *what?*"

"Hear me out. There's an unprecedented interest in the paranormal right now. Every other film or tv show that comes out deals with the supernatural, and the cultural obsession just seems to be growing. So – we buy shitty houses like this, houses that can't find a buyer due to their reputation for being haunted, market them *specifically* to those with an obsessive interest in the supernatural, and sell them for a massive profit without even having to put a lick of paint on the place!"

Mike stared, open mouthed, then turned away again to gesture aggressively at their surroundings. "Fucking *ghosts??* *This* is your big fucking idea?? *This* is why you told me not to tell anyone where I was going, or with who? You think someone might *steal* this stupid fucking idea? You're a fucking idiot! Ever heard that old joke? 'How can you tell if your house is haunted? Simple: *it isn't.*' Fuckwit!"

"It's a winner. And I'm offering you a partnership."

Mike snorted. "Partnership?? You must be—" A thought suddenly occurred. "You haven't already bought this place, have you?"

The floorboards creaked as Jacob walked up behind Mike. "Sure have."

"Oh, for fuck's sake!" Mike dug into his pocket and pulled out his phone. "What's the address? Never mind, I've got it. You're fucking crazy if you think I'm buying into this, literally *or* figuratively! You can take your partnership offer and—"

"Yeah, well, that's not the sort of partnership I had in mind…"

"And look!" Mike stabbed a finger at the screen of his phone. "There's not a single fucking mention online of this place even having a *reputation* for being haunted!"

"Well, no," said Jacob. "That's because it isn't."

Something dropped past Mike's face, and as the wire began to cut into his neck, he heard Jacob say: "Not *yet*, anyway…"

The Precious One

"Shh, Precious..." David clutched the boy to his breast, whispering as he pressed himself into the shadows, peering around the partially collapsed brick wall as the shouting of the scavengers drifted down the alleyway from the road beyond.

Almost made it all the way home. At least they'd lost his trail, else they'd have swarmed down here already, all sharpened teeth and glass blades.

The sounds grew momentarily louder, then muffled, then loud again, the queer angles of fallen buildings channelling their voices in ways that would never have occurred when the city lived. Scavengers rarely ventured into dark, restricted spaces that might hide an ambush, but David knew bravado might still send one of them creeping down here.

He shifted uncomfortably, tightening his grip on his precious burden. The boy slumped against him, limp and pallid, eyes closed, and David was hyper-aware of the meds stashed in his pocket. He had to move. Had to get home quickly.

The scavengers sounded distant now, and he hoped the local acoustics were on his side. With quiet, precise steps he began to pick his way across the rubble towards the mouth of the alley, a rectangle of twilight tinged with that faint glow from the crater at the centre of the city. David paused as he reached it, sticking his head out into the road beyond and glancing about, then ducking back into darkness. Distant-sounding voices drifted on the breeze, but there'd been nobody in sight.

David adjusted his hold on the boy. *Across the road, down the side-street opposite, turn right into the laneway, up the fire ladder—* That was going to be hard. Maybe sling the boy over his shoulder, so he could use both hands to climb? But if the boy slipped…

"Come on, Precious. Hold tight."

Bracing himself, David scuttled forward, skipping around piles of debris and hurdling waterlogged potholes as he darted towards the shadows of the side street.

There was a sudden shout from somewhere behind him.

Dammit! He doubled his pace, substituting speed for any precision. He didn't glance back, but knew they'd be swarming after him already. Grasping the boy tightly enough to bruise them both, he ran for his life, quickly reaching the side street and pelting along it.

More shouts, far too close.

Drop the boy.

He shook his head vehemently.

They'd be satisfied with that.

NO! He ran on, hearing his pursuers round the corner behind him as he reached the laneway and hurled himself into the slim passageway between buildings. The fire ladder, bolted to the wall just metres away, caught the dying rays of the sun.

No time to stop. Still running, David let go of the boy, grabbing the child's ankle by one hand as he fell and using the momentum to swing the boy up and over his shoulder, leaving David's other hand free to grab the bottom rung of the ladder. With a desperate prayer, David released his hold on the boy altogether and began to pull himself up the ladder, rung by painful rung. *If I can just get to the mid-point and pull the ladder up—*

Screams of excitement from below told David he was too late. He risked a glance downwards, and saw that one of his pursuers had already escaped the scrum at the bottom of the ladder and was climbing up after him. David looked up again. Just five more rungs to the sixth-floor window. *Four. Three—*

A hand gouged against his worn boots, fingers seeking purchase. David slammed a foot down, and heard a scream as fingers were crushed between metal and rubber. He could feel the boy beginning to slide off his shoulders as his hand found the windowsill. Hooking his fingers into the rotting wood, he heaved himself up, bucking the boy forwards and over his head like a rodeo horse. They both spilled through the window and into the dusty-dark landing of the interior stairwell. Immediately pushing the boy aside, David scrambled to his feet, reaching for the pile of bricks stacked by the window. Gripping one tightly, he glanced out the window, looking back down the ladder. The scavenger had almost reached them. David steeped to the side, into the shadows, and waited. Heard the sounds of pursuit change from climbing to scrabbling. Rough, bloodied fingers gripped the sill, then a sweaty, red face appeared. Bloodshot eyes fell upon the boy, and a broken-toothed mouth twisted into a leer of hunger and triumph.

"DON'T YOU TOUCH MY BOY!" David screamed, and swung his arm around, driving the brick into the face as hard as he could.

Flesh and bone gave under the blow. With a grunt of surprise, the scavenger fell backwards and out of sight. David didn't bother to look as he quickly gathered up the boy and charged up the stairs towards the fifteenth floor, where the exposed girders would provide a bridge to the next building, and the safety of apartment 221B—but the sudden shocked silence from the laneway, followed by gleeful shouting, told him everything he needed to know about his pursuer's fate…

Kendra let him in, then helped get the boy to the kitchen and lay him down on the Formica tabletop. She stroked the boy's cheek. "Hey, Precious..." Then she looked at David. "Got the meds?"

David fished the pills from his pocket. "They threw them in."

"How much all up?"

"Too much. But at least Steve never cuts meds with other shit."

They popped their pills dry. David leaned against the table, trembling slightly.

"Feeling the rads?"

He shook his head. "No more than usual. Chased by scavengers. Almost lost him." He nodded towards the boy.

Kendra touched David's arm, then turned to pick up a large knife from the counter. "You rest a bit. I'll get dinner."

He smiled weakly. "Love you."

"Love *you*," she replied. Then, with practiced movements, she began to remove the boy's forearm at the joint.

Story Acknowledgements

'Daddy's Always Right' © Chuck McKenzie.
First published in AntipodeanSF, 2022. Ed. Ion Newcombe.

'Conquest' © Chuck McKenzie.
First published in AntipodeanSF, 2002. Ed. Ion Newcombe.

'Kindred' © Chuck McKenzie. Original to this collection.

'Literality' © Chuck McKenzie.
First published in AurealisXpress, 2004.

'Moth' © Chuck McKenzie.
First published in AntipodeanSF, 2006. Ed. Ion Newcombe.

'Catfish' © Chuck McKenzie. First published in Daily Grind and Other
Astounding Stories of Mundane Matters, 2024, Daft Notions.

'Bad Meat' © Chuck McKenzie. First published in Andromeda Spaceways
Inflight Magazine, 2010. Ed. Felicity Dowker.

'Tenant' © Chuck McKenzie.
First published in AntipodeanSF, 2024. Ed. Ion Newcombe.

'Daily Grind' © Chuck McKenzie.
First published in Infinitas Bookshop Newsletter, 2004.

'Old Habits Die' © Chuck McKenzie.
First published in AntipodeanSF, 2001. Ed. Ion Newcomb.

'New Tricks' © Chuck McKenzie.
First published in AntipodeanSF, 2025. Ed. Ion Newcombe.

'What Goes Uptime' © Chuck McKenzie.
First published in AntipodeanSF, 2006. Ed. Ion Newcombe.

'Closing the Loop' © Chuck McKenzie. Original to this collection.

About the Author
CHUCK McKENZIE

Chuck McKenzie was born way back in the 20th Century, and is still not dead, allegedly. He writes stuff. You can stalk him on Instagram at **@chuck.mckenzie.author**

Also By
CHUCK McKENZIE

Worlds Apart (Novel, Hybrid Publishers 1999)

AustrAlien Absurdities: Comic Tales of Science-Fiction, Fantasy & Horror by Australian Authors (Anthology, co-edited with Tansy Rayner-Roberts, Agog! Press 2001)

Confessions of a Pod Person (Collection, MirrorDanse Editions 2005)

Conversations With My Cat (Collection, co-authored with MacReady McKenzie and Ripley McKenzie, Daft Notions 2023)

The Dark Man, By Referral and Less Pleasant Tales (Collection, Daft Notions 2024)

All I Want For Christmas (Novella, Daft Notions 2024)

Daily Grind and Other Astounding Stories of Mundane Matters (Collection, Daft Notions 2024)

Time Spent With A Cat (Novella, Daft Notions 2024)

Alien Space Nazis Must Die! (Novella, Daft Notions 2024)

The Dark Man, By Referral (Novella, Daft Notions 2024)

Conversations With Dog (Collection, Daft Notions 2025)

Also By

CHUCK McKENZIE
THE DARK MAN, BY REFERRAL
AND LESS PLEASANT TALES

*STEP INTO THE WORLD
OF THE DARK MAN:*

*PLEASE HAVE YOUR
REFERRAL READY...*

An abused child encounters the local legendary boogeyman,
and finds himself querying the definition of 'monster'...

Two time-travellers observe The Crucifixion, and discover a horror
far beyond the brutality of the event itself...

An inhuman predator establishes its feeding ground in a small rural town
—but does it have competition...?

In this collection, representing the darker work of author
Chuck McKenzie, you'll find tales of zombies, kaiju,
and alien invaders; of visits to Hell, and to quiet suburban streets;
of Lovecraftian entities and spectral terrors.

And other, far less pleasant tales than these...

Also By

CHUCK McKENZIE

DAILY GRIND

AND OTHER ASTOUNDING STORIES OF MUNDANE MATTERS

THE DIFFERENCE BETWEEN THE EVERYDAY AND THE ASTOUNDING DEPENDS ENTIRELY UPON YOUR VIEWPOINT...

A conversation between two aliens reveals that some aspects of working life are universal, such as job satisfaction—or the lack thereof...

A private detective investigates an impossible murder, unwillingly assisted by an annoyingly talkative cat who may or may not be completely imaginary...

A daring hero defiantly battles Alien Space Nazis for the fate of the galaxy—but doesn't it all seem just little bit...unlikely....?

In this collection, comprising the science fiction stories (including three novellas) of author Chuck McKenzie, you'll find tales of time-travellers, interstellar scam artists, and interdimensional expeditions; of alien invaders masquerading as Santa, and others offering services that sound too good to be true; of bushrangers battling Wellsian Martians, and the unthinkable results of doubling the average human lifespan.

And other astounding stories of relatively mundane matters...

Also By
CHUCK McKENZIE
TIME SPENT WITH A CAT

Time Spent With A Cat: the best Hard SF gonzo-fantasy murder-mystery novella featuring a possibly-imaginary talking cat you'll ever read, probably.

My name's Jim Carpenter. I'm a private eye.
And business has been in the toilet since everyone found themselves saddled with an ethereal entity that floats beside them. Mine is a wiseass talking cat. I hate cats.
But's that's not my biggest problem, because a cashed-up frenemy from my military days has just given me six hours to solve the murder of a scientist who was working on something very special for the Special Weapons Division. Shot in the head, only one possible killer, witnesses on the scene within seconds.

Should be an easy case, right?

Except that, impossibly, the weapon and bullet have both vanished.

And the clock is ticking.

Also By
CHUCK McKENZIE
ALL I WANT FOR CHRISTMAS

++the g'norr are
your friends —
welcome them — love,
serve, obey++

It's Christmastime, and a full-scale covert alien invasion is underway!

Bullied back into service, retired g'norr squadleader Sneet must help claim the primitive planet Earth for the glory of the G'norr Dominion by undertaking a mission that involves brainwashing human children in preparation for the takeover… all while working undercover as a shopping mall Santa.

With the might and technology of a galaxy-spanning extraterrestrial empire pitted against a bunch of primitive juvenile primates, nothing could possibly go wrong. Right?
Right…?

Also By

CHUCK McKENZIE
ALIEN SPACE NAZIS MUST DIE!

When the evil forces of the Alien Space Nazis threaten the galaxy, there's only one man smart enough, tough enough, and sassy enough to defeat them! Lars Jansen! Whether it's escaping from a Nazi KillMoon seconds before it explodes, battling monsters in a combat pit, or dispatching entire legions of alien troopers armed only with a pocket knife, it's all in a day's work for this swashbuckling hero!

Which, when you think about it, all seems a bit...unlikely. Doesn't it?

Also By
CHUCK McKENZIE
THE DARK MAN, BY REFERRAL

So what is a monster anyway...?

James had always believed the Dark Man was just an urban myth. A legendary monster. A small-town boogeyman used by adults to keep kids in line.

But then he discovered that the Dark Man was very real indeed, and that the definition of 'monster' very much depended upon one's point of view...

Also By

CHUCK McKENZIE

CONVERSATIONS WITH MY CAT

Feed me?

What does Schrödinger's Cat have to do with a chewed computer cord? How do you fit work around a cat's napping schedule? Why do cats change their minds as soon as you open the door for them?

These and other conundrums are addressed in this collection of discussions between one man and his cat, wherein are tackled many of the greatest issues of our time: politics, religion, culture, history, human rights, and poop.

You'll laugh, you'll cry, it'll change your life. Or not. Frankly, we'll say anything to get you to buy this book, which is – fair warning – NOT FOR KIDS, as the cat featured herein is a real pottymouth.

Also By

CHUCK McKENZIE

CONVERSATIONS WITH DOG

Can dogs really sense ghosts, or are they just taking the piss? What is it about the 'W' word (walkies) that makes dogs go absolutely apeshit? Are there any canine attributes that would count as transferrable skills if a dog applied for a job?

These, and other issues you never really gave a crap about, are addressed in this blatant cash-grab masquerading as a sequel to the mildly-popular Conversations With My Cat, as Chuck McKenzie discusses the complexities of life and leashes with the dog down the road.

'By equal measures utterly hilarious and terribly sad,' is how the teller describes Chuck's bank balance, so please buy this book.

Sci-Fi, Horror, Crime and...Cats?

Small press publisher operating out of
Melbourne, Australia.

For more information and to purchase our titles go to:
www.daftnotions.com